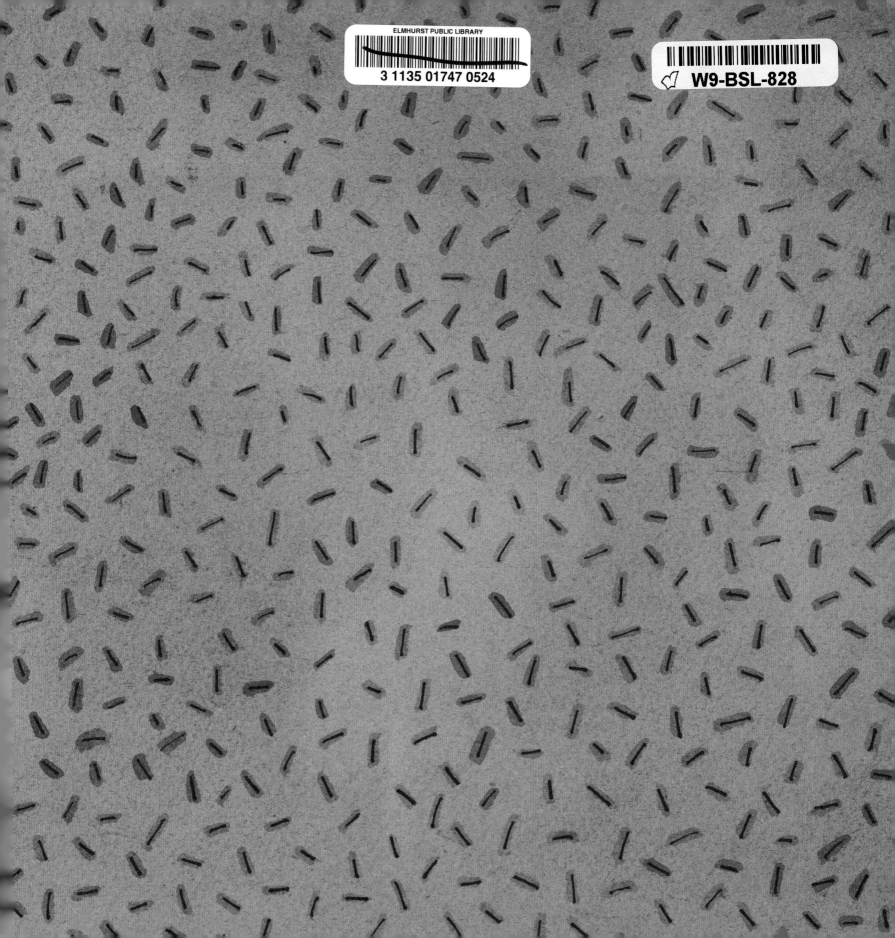

That Cat Can't Stay

Written by Thad Krasnesky

Illustrated by David Parkins

Flash
Light PRESS

To Barret, Dublin, Bella, Olivia, and Breve, the inspiration for this story,
and my daughters, Rachael and Isabelle. —TK

For Lisa and Alan, but mostly for Lauren. So good to have you with us. —DP

Copyright © 2010 by Flashlight Press
Text copyright © 2010 by Thad Krasnesky
Illustrations copyright © 2010 by David Parkins
All rights reserved, including the right of reproduction, in whole or in part, in any form.
Printed in China.
First Edition — April 2010
Library of Congress Control Number: 2009939020
ISBN 978-0-9799746-5-6
Editor: Shari Dash Greenspan
Graphic Design: The Virtual Paintbrush
This book was typeset in Centaur.
The illustrations were rendered in pen & ink and watercolor.
Distributed by Independent Publishers Group
Flashlight Press • 527 Empire Blvd. • Brooklyn, NY 11225
www.FlashlightPress.com

When Mom brought home a stray one day,

Dad said, "That creature cannot stay.
There's no use begging.
Don't say please.
I don't like cats.
They scratch my knees.
    And I don't want to have to shout,
        so kindly put
            that cat-thing out."

Mom said, "I'll put him back outside.
I'm sure he'll find some place to hide,
away from all the rain and hail
which just might drench him, nose to tail.
I see you do not want this pet
though he might get completely wet.
Your mind's made up, dear, I can tell.
I'll put him out."
      But Dad said, "Well…

…the rain
is coming down
so hard.
There's not
a dry spot
in the yard.
I guess
the cat
can stay in here
until
this rainstorm
starts to clear…

…but NO ONE pet him! DO NOT play!
My mind's made up.
        That cat can't stay!"

The day Mom found a calico,
Dad said, "That thing has got to go.
One cat was more than I could take.
Two cats would be a big mistake!
    There's no use begging.
    Don't say please.
    I don't like cats.
    They scratch my knees.
    They carry fleas.
    They make me sneeze.
    They're always getting
    stuck in trees.
I want it gone. Vamoose! Away!
I'm telling you,
    that cat can't stay."

"All right," said Mom, "She's beautiful,
but you're quite right. Our house is full.
I'll put her back out on the street.
She'll have to scrounge for things to eat.
But she'll survive. Yes, I can tell.
I'll put her out."

But Dad said, "Well...

…we'll feed her for a day or two,
but after that – I'm warning you –
when she has gained a little weight,
she's out of here. There's no debate.
We cannot keep another stray.
You mark my words:
that cat can't stay!"

When we were in the parking lot,
Mom called, "Hey kids! Look what I've got!"
Dad said, "Don't show me what you've found.
We don't need one more cat around.

There's no use begging.
Don't say please.
I don't like cats.
They scratch my knees.
They carry fleas.
They make me sneeze.
They're always getting stuck in trees.

They eat my cheese.
They hairball-wheeze.
Their licking makes my stomach quease.
Three cats?
    We do not have the space.
    She'll have to find another place."

"You're right again," Mom said to Dad, "and I won't cry or get too sad
just thinking of this little cat and how a car might squish her flat.
Abandoned in this parking lot, 'slim chance to none' is all she's got.
Poor cat, just go. You heard the boss.
But look both ways before you cross.
It won't help to meow or yell.
Just watch for traffic."
Dad said, "Well…

…perhaps we'll drive her out a bit to someplace where she won't get hit.
We'll even show her picture 'round and put up posters saying FOUND!
Now kids, sit down and stop that 'yay'-ing.
THIS cat's NOT — you hear? — not staying."

One night my mom rushed in the door from doing errands at the store.
"This ginger kitty has been hit,
so I got out and rescued it."
Dad said, "UN-rescue it, my dear.
We have no room
for four cats here.

There's no use begging.
Don't say please.

I don't like cats.
They scratch my knees.

They make me sneeze.

They carry fleas.

They're always getting
stuck in trees.

They eat my cheese.

They hairball-wheeze.

Their licking makes
my stomach quease.

I'm sure that everyone agrees: WE CAN'T HAVE ANY MORE OF THESE!"

Mom softly said, "I'm sure you're right. I'll send him back into the night.
His leg is broken. He can't walk. He's easy pickings for a hawk.
Poor thing, it will be over soon. I doubt he'll make it through till noon.
 So, best of luck there, little fella.
 Go outside now."
 Dad said, "Well, uh...

…if his leg is truly broken, maybe I've too harshly spoken.
Take him to the vet tonight to see if she can set it right.
But when he's well, without delay,
that cat moves out.
That cat can't stay!"

When I was coming home from school
I broke the "no more kitties" rule.
I hid the tabby in my hood
because I knew my father would
not let me bring her in the house
though she was tiny as a mouse.
I knew just what my dad would say —

"Another cat? That cat can't stay."

There's no use begging. Don't say please. I don't like cats. They scratch my knees. They carry fleas. They make me sneeze. They're always getting stuck in

trees. They eat my cheese. They hairball-wheeze. Their licking makes my stomach quease. I'm sure that EVERYONE agrees: we can't have ANY more of these!"

So I kissed Dad and I said, "Pleeeease…

...could you just give her
one small squeeze?"

That week, Dad said, "Look what I found all sad and lonely at the pound."

And we were happy to discover…

...Daddy is a doggy lover!

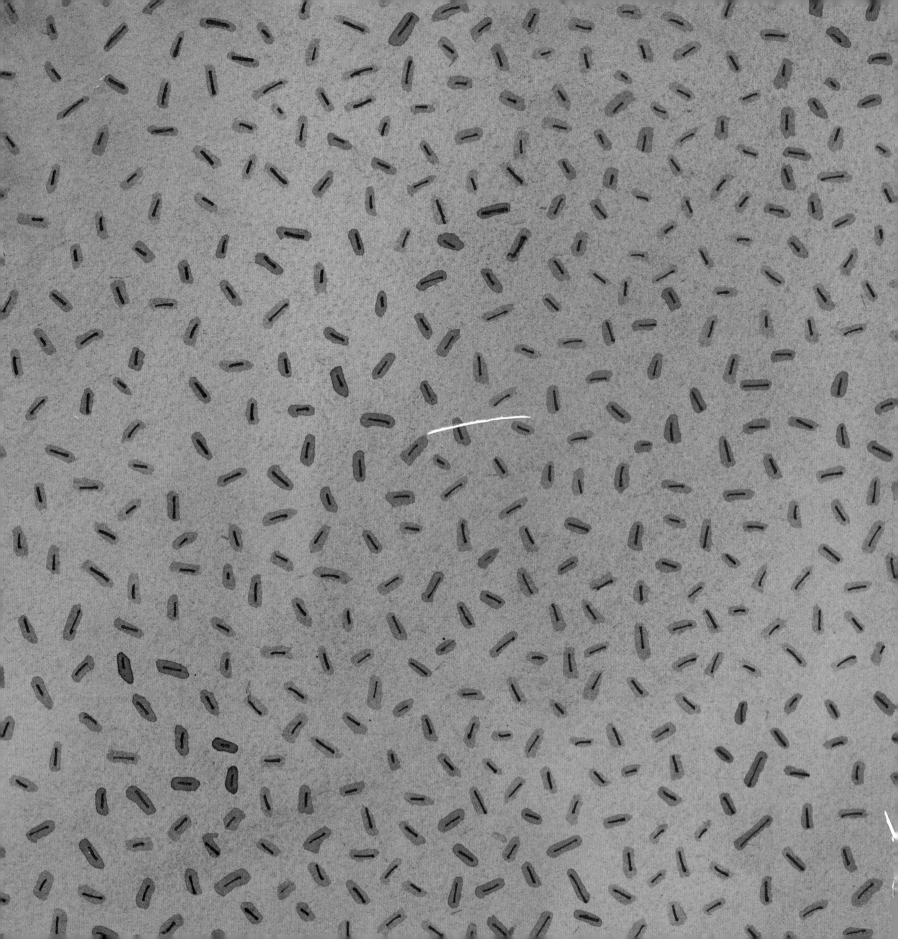